THE
SHIPWRECK

To Peter — J. R.
To Richard Bowgen. Thanks for being such a great uncle! With love — H. C.

This translation has been sponsored by the Danish Arts Council
Committee for Literature. The publisher wishes to thank John Mason for
his work on the translation of this story and the Danish Arts Council for
their generous support.

Barefoot Books
2067 Massachusetts Ave
Cambridge, MA 02140

© Gaïa Editions
Text copyright © 1979 by Jørn Riel
Illustrations copyright © 2011 by Helen Cann
The moral rights of Jørn Riel and Helen Cann have been asserted

First published in the United States by Barefoot Books, Inc in 2011

Translation by John Mason
Graphic design by Graham Webb, Design Principals, Warminster, UK
Reproduction by B & P International, Hong Kong
Printed in China on 100% acid-free paper by Printplus, Ltd
This book was typeset in Cleanhouse and Avenir
The illustrations were prepared in watercolor, graphite and collage

Library of Congress Cataloging-in-Publication Data is available under
LCCN 2010041871

ISBN 978-1-84686-335-6

1 3 5 7 9 8 6 4 2

THE
SHIPWRECK

Written by Jørn Riel

Illustrated by Helen Cann

Barefoot Books
step inside a story

Contents

1. Leiv

Leiv Steinursson laughed on the day that his father was killed. On the family farm, Leiv had tied a string between the well and stable door, and Uncle Helge tripped right over it and tumbled head first into a steaming fresh cowpat. Leiv laughed so loud it echoed around the buildings of the farm at Stockanæs, then he leapt up onto the turf roof of the sheepfold, where he knew his uncle could not pursue him.

But that same evening, when his father's men brought the news of how Thorstein had sliced Steinur's head off, Leiv was not laughing any more. He bit into his lip to stop himself from sobbing like his younger brothers and sisters. He went outside and stood next to his horse, Flax, in the low-beamed stable, where he

swore a terrible revenge on Thorstein, then wept until Flax's neck was soaked with his tears.

For several months, Leiv did not mention his father. The boy whose skylarking had always made him the terror of the farm became strangely quiet and obedient. His mother grew worried and often spoke to Uncle Helge about the change that had come over Leiv. And Helge promised to take the boy with him to Norway the following summer. But that was not how things turned out.

The day Thorstein was sentenced by the gathering of elders to three years exile from Iceland, Leiv vanished from the farm.

Thorstein Gunnarsson had resolved to spend his exile on Greenland. He loaded his men on three small skiffs along with their beasts and chattels and set sail from Gunnarsnæs early one morning in July. Also on board Thorstein's skiff was Leiv, concealed among the sheep. It was only when the boats were out on the open sea that he stepped forward, declared himself and challenged Thorstein.

Lovers of a good fight, the massive Icelanders hooted with laughter. This little pip-squeak, this chip off Steinur's block, so impudently daring to square up to Thorstein! They stared at the lad standing in their midst, his chin jutting, his body quivering with the lust for battle before the gigantic figure of Thorstein Gunnarsson, and they fell about laughing.

Thorstein fixed them with a look that made the laughter freeze on their large, flushed faces. Then he turned his eyes on Leiv.

"You've got courage," he said, "and I like to fight men of courage. But I cannot accept your challenge. There is peace between our families, and there must continue to be."

Leiv raised his sword. It was called Stonecleaver and it had been given to him by his Uncle Helge.

"You killed my father, so I have to kill you," he said.

"I did kill your father." Thorstein nodded. "But your father killed my brother and two of his men. That is why I had to do it. My penance is to go into exile for three years."

"I have to kill you anyway," answered Leiv.

Thorstein laid his hand on Leiv's sword.

"That sounds reasonable," he said. "But I think you should wait a few years. Until your arms have grown as long as mine."

Leiv gripped Stonecleaver's hilt with both hands and lifted the sword above his head. One of Thorstein's men rushed forward and grabbed hold of it by the point. With a quick movement Leiv brought the sword down, and the iron blade cut into the man's fingers.

With a roar, Thorstein stopped his men in their tracks, just as they were about to throw themselves upon Leiv.

"Leave him be!" he shouted. "He did what any of us would have done." Then he turned to Leiv. "Why did you creep on board my boat?"

"Because I knew that you wouldn't be able to run away from me once we were out at sea," replied Leiv.

Once again the crew laughed. The thought of Thorstein Gunnarsson running away from Leiv was almost too much. Even Thorstein had to suppress a smile.

"Hmm…I see. Well, that was good thinking. Out here, you are right, I cannot run away. I can see no way around it. You'll have to stay onboard. That way you'll know where you've got me, and when your arms have grown as long as mine, then we can settle our little score. What do you say to that?"

Leiv took his time to ponder the matter.

"How long will it take?"

"If you mean your arms, that'll take a few years yet. But as for our duel, I'd say it'll be over pretty quickly." Thorstein looked down at Leiv, with a glint in his eyes.

Leiv considered this answer. Of course he'd prefer to kill Thorstein on the spot. Then he could put this business behind him and go back to the farm and help his mother and Uncle Helge. But on the other hand it might not be so easy to fell this giant. It was an awfully long way up to Thorstein's head, and his neck was as thick as a tree trunk. It would take a pair of long, strong arms to bring him down.

"Well, that had best be that, then," he mumbled at last and slipped the sword back into its leather sheath.

Thorstein held out his hand, and Leiv took it. There was now a pact between the two of them, and a pact could not be broken by either party. Thorstein released his hand and put an arm around Leiv's shoulder.

"You can help the men on deck," he said. "That way you'll learn a bit about seamanship."

Leiv nodded. He looked up, and his eyes met Thorstein's. They were very blue and friendly and surrounded with a tracery of thin laughter lines. "It's a pity," he thought, "that Thorstein was forced to kill my father. That means that I have to kill him. But such is the unwritten law and there is not much I can do about it."

2. Narua and Apuluk

Her name was Narua, which means "seagull." She was only eleven years old, and laughing had always come easier to her than crying. Narua had two brothers. A baby brother, who was still so small that he was mostly carried in a sling on his mother's back, and a big brother, who was twelve. His name was Apuluk.

There were a lot of children in the settlement, for the tribe was a large one, and for many years now there had been no famine at all. When the hungry years came, her grandfather Shinka had told her, it was the custom to leave newborn baby girls outside for the wolves or the foxes. It was better to be without girls than boys. Boys would grow up to be hunters one day.

Narua was glad that she had not been left outside,

for she loved being alive. She divided her time between helping her mother and playing. What she liked best was playing with Apuluk, but Apuluk did not always have time to play with his little sister. He was so big now that once in a while he went out hunting with the grown men. When he was eleven, he had caught his first seal all by himself, and that had been a sign that he would soon be grown up.

Neither Narua nor Apuluk knew that they were living on the world's largest island. They called themselves Inuit, which means *humans*, and their country was called Inuit Nunat, The Land of Humans. The children knew that the country was vast, for they were always traveling. The

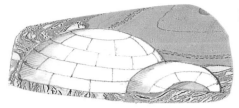

Inuit were nomads: they moved from place to place without having any fixed place to stay. They built houses out of stone and turf, in which they spent the winter — large, warm houses each with space for several families.

When they traveled in winter they built igloos — small, round huts of snow, which were so strong that you could drive a fully laden sled over the top of them.

In summer, the Inuit moved into tents made of sealskins sewn together.

Narua and Apuluk's grandfather was called Shinka. He was a great storyteller, with a memory that was better than most of the other elders'. In winter, when it was dark for most of the day, time often hung heavy. That was when Shinka began to tell his stories. He told of the Moonman, who was called Kilaq, and of the mythical animal Kilivpak, which was bigger than a bear. It was such a strange creature that, once it had been caught and its meat had been eaten, new meat immediately began to grow out of its gnawed bones.

Shinka knew an amazing number of stories and never told the same one twice, unless he was asked to do so. He had heard these stories from his father, who had in turn heard them from his, and the children understood that these stories were just as ancient as the Inuit themselves.

When Shinka told them about the mighty inland dwellers, who were twice as big as ordinary people and who boiled the Inuit they caught in huge pots, the children shivered. Shinka's stories made them afraid of venturing too far up into the valleys when they went looking for berries, and they kept at a good distance from the great ice mass that stretched like a giant's backbone behind the cliffs that lined the shores. When Shinka told them something frightening, Narua and Apuluk liked to creep behind their father and lean their foreheads into his back. They felt safe like this, for no one was as strong and invincible as their father.

The children and their families were always on the move. And they liked it. They moved from house to house, from fjord to fjord. Traveling was their way of life. They found their security in their mother and father, their brothers and sisters, their relatives. They slept together, ate together and spent most of their time together. The children knew nothing of clock time. They slept when they were tired; they often played well into the small hours, ate when they were hungry and worked when they felt like it. Maybe that is why Inuit children grew up to be happy and contented people.

3. The Foreign Ships

One spring, Apuluk and Narua moved with the tribe to a beautiful fjord that they called Simiutat, which means "corks." They gave it this name because across the mouth of the fjord lay a clump of small islands, jammed together like a cork in a bottle.

It was a lovely fjord, long and narrow with high slopes rising on either side of the water. Foaming torrents flowed from the inland ice in abundance; the long tributary valleys were rich in flowers and berries, and best of all there was plenty of game both in the water and on land.

Once the place where they would make their summer settlement had been chosen, Narua and Apuluk lent a hand in emptying the umiak, the women's boat. There were many things that had to be carried ashore. First were the dogs, which had been lying with their legs bound so that they would not fight. The long sea voyage had made their joints stiff, but not so stiff that they could not throw themselves into a huge fight as soon as they felt firm ground beneath their paws.

Then there were all the domestic items that had to be carried up above the high-water mark — skins and clothing, pots and bowls, and wood for the meat frames. Last of all they dragged the great tents up the slope that led to the water. Here the tents were pitched so that each entrance faced the fjord. The children were worn out but when the early hours of the morning came, they could at last lie down to sleep.

That summer something strange happened. One day, when Narua and Apuluk had gone up the mountain to gather herbs for pickling blubber, they caught sight of a peculiar ship sailing toward them far out at sea.

At first they were terribly frightened, for they

thought that it was a sea monster, one of the many grotesque creatures that Shinka had told them about. But soon they saw that the boat was made roughly in the same way as an umiak, only many times larger. They also noticed that there was a great pole growing up through the middle of the ship and that on the pole was stretched a huge white skin.

The children flattened themselves into the grass and followed the ship with fearful eyes. They could see living beings on board, and they could hear the shouting of voices that sounded almost like Inuit voices. Narua whispered to Apuluk that they might be inland dwellers, who had built a mighty umiak and were now traveling around gathering Inuit for their huge pots. Apuluk shook his head. He had heard that the inland dwellers did not like water. That was why they lived so far from the coast.

Once the ship had disappeared behind the farthest of the islands in the neck of the fjord, the children sprang up and ran home.

That evening, they told their father what they had

seen from the uplands. He listened to them with a serious face and nodded in confirmation.

"This kind of boat has been talked about," he said. "A seal hunter from Katla's tribe once encountered such a boat when he was on his way home from Agpat."

"Are they inland dwellers?" asked Narua.

Her father shook his head.

"No, they are a people we know nothing about. They sail across the sea from the south and come ashore here on our coasts. The man from Katla's tribe said that these people could be very fearsome. He said they had sliced a hunter in half with a huge knife made of a material his people had never used."

The next day four men from the tribe rowed out to see if they could spot the foreign boat. Narua and Apuluk watched the kayaks disappear. Their father rowed at the head, and they saw him turn and look back toward the coast before he disappeared behind the islands.

"What if he doesn't come back?" whispered Narua.

"Imagine if the strangers catch him and slice him in half."

Apuluk shook his head.

"They can't catch Father," he said. "He can creep right up without them seeing him, and even if they do catch sight of him, he can easily row away from their big, clumsy boat."

He got up and they set off homewards.

"Did you know there were other people apart from us, Apuluk?"

"No." Apuluk struck the grass with his harpoon. "Of course, we can't be sure they are real people, like you and me. Maybe they are some kind of spirit that we know nothing about. We can ask Grandfather."

But Shinka knew nothing about the strangers. He only knew about the old spirits, who had lived with the Inuit for many centuries. And he was certain that the seal hunter in Katla's tribe was lying.

26

But it looked as
though there had
been some truth
in the story after all.

When the kayaks
returned, the four hunters had many things to recount
about the mysterious ship and its crew. They had
come upon it deep in a fjord just a day's journey from
the settlement.

The mighty tree trunk that the children had seen had
been lowered, and they had seen many beings that
resembled the Inuit: men and women and children.
However, these creatures were different from ordinary
people. They had hair the color of the yellow poppy,

and almost all the men had long and unruly beards they had never seen before. It was truly a strange and threatening visit here in the Land of Humans.

The hunters had not attempted to sail right up to the ship, for many of these strangers on the shore could easily have spotted the kayaks. They had seen something that looked like houses on land, and they had also seen strange creatures, one of which looked a little like a musk ox and another like a reindeer.

All night long, the adults in the group sat and talked about this extraordinary new event. Narua and Apuluk lay in their sleeping sacks listening carefully. It was, they thought, so exciting that there were people in the world other than Inuit, and quite amazing that these people had found their way up to the Land of Humans.

The following day, two more of these big ships were observed on their way north. They sailed so close to the shore that from their hiding places on land the Inuit could see the animals and people on board.

In the interests of safety the elders decided that the summer settlement should be moved. The strangers could make unpleasant neighbors, if Katla's reports were to be trusted. So the tents were taken down and they sailed out of Simiutat and farther south.

Narua and Apuluk were a little sorry to be leaving these newcomers behind. Maybe they were not as dangerous as they had been made out to be. So little was known about them. They did not even know whether they spoke the language of humans.

They traveled for four days before finding a place that the hunters considered to be good. There they established a settlement and lived as they had at Simiutat.

Narua often thought about the strange boats she had seen. But, once autumn came and they moved to their winter settlement even farther south, she came to forget her experience of the summer.

Almost a whole year was to pass before she and Apuluk would see anything of the people from the strange ships again.

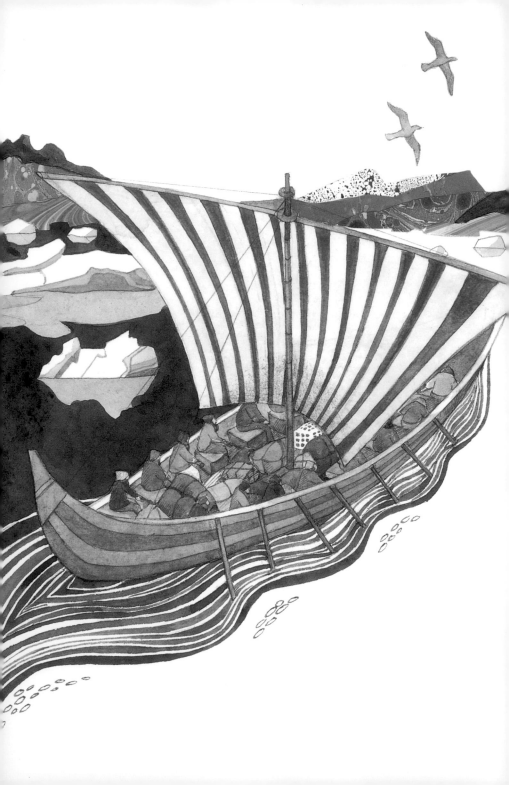

4. Shipwreck

Thorstein was an accomplished seafarer. He had been to Greenland before, and kinsmen of his had lived there for over a hundred years. He steered the skiff with the aid of a pelorus and the North Star.

There was no proper cabin on the skiff. There was just one raised platform fore and one aft, and between these two platforms was a deep well where the cargo was stashed.

The two other boats followed Thorstein. They were never so far away that they could not shout to each other. This far north it may be light day and night, but freezing fog can quickly come rolling in along the coast of Greenland. Then everything depends on being within hailing distance of each other

The channel between Iceland and Greenland usually holds no dangers in summer. Big storms seldom sweep across it and visibility is generally good. In the autumn and winter, on the other hand, it can be a risky business setting sail. During these seasons it is dark for most of the day, and the storms roll in one after the other. Many Viking ships had lost their bearings because of a sudden snowstorm, and even more had gone down in the enormous waves whipped up by the powerful winds.

Leiv had not been on board for many days before his usual high spirits returned. He had postponed vengeance to some day in the future. Meanwhile, he got on well with Thorstein. Much of the time he spent at the top of the mast as lookout, and it was usually he who alerted the crew when seals or whales came into sight.

When they had been at sea for a week, the weather suddenly turned nasty. An icy wind blew from the northeast, and powerful gusts made the mast creak and stretched the sail to bursting point.

Thorstein looked up at the sky with anxious eyes. He gave his men orders to cover over the well of the skiff so that there was a place where animals and people would not be soaked to the skin.

The wind gathered force. Violent squalls of rain and hail lashed the boat, and the men pulled their homespun coats up over their heads and cursed the unseasonal summer weather. Leiv stood beside Thorstein. He had a shield over his head, for the hailstones were almost as big as cherries and, where they hit, they hit hard.

"Are we going under?" Leiv asked.

Thorstein shook his head.

"The wind cannot hurt us," he growled. "It's the ice I am afraid of." He pointed out across the heaving sea. "We are not far from the ice. I can hear it."

Leiv listened but he could hear nothing above the roar of the storm.

All the loose cargo was lashed down so as not to be blown into the sea. Thorstein had the sail lowered and set his men to the oars so that the bows of the boat

could be held into the wind.

All night they rowed, but the merciless wind kept up. Leiv slogged at the oar until his shoulders ached, and the men cursed and rowed as though possessed in order to hold their course. The women and children who had come with them sat under the large tarpaulins deep in the hold among the animals. Early the next morning the lookout shouted that he could see pieces of floating ice. It was blue ice, which is especially dangerous as it is hard to see in the water. Thorstein ordered his men to row harder, but he soon realized that they could not row away from the drifting ice. Within a matter of hours, huge floes of ice had caught up with them and surrounded them on all sides. The sea grew calm as the waves were stilled by the mass of ice coming from the east coast of Greenland. It began to grind

34

frighteningly against the sides of the boat. All three boats lay in the midst of a broad belt of ice stretching as far as the eye could see, with the ice floes pressing in from all sides. The heavy planks of the skiff began to buckle dangerously.

The men drew in their oars and leaned over the side of the boat. In some places, a plank had stoved in and water was streaming in through the cracks. They stuffed canvas soaked in wax into the cracks and bailed out continuously.

Thorstein's skiff had the worst of it. It had sprung a leak in the keel and, despite constant bailing, the water continued to rise in the hold.

"We'll have to try to get over into the other boats!" he shouted.

Leiv grabbed him by the arm.

"I can jump across to them over the ice floes," he said.

Thorstein looked down at him with furrowed brows. Then he nodded.

"Tell them to try to get as close

to us as possible. Otherwise we'll never get the animals on board."

Leiv leapt down onto the ice. He ran from floe to floe, leaping across broad cracks of black water. All the time he could feel the ice rocking under him. Several times he fell and found himself sliding until he learned how to use his hands and nails as a brake to stop himself.

Even before he had reached the nearest boat, the worst possible thing happened. The fog came rolling in, and in the space of a few seconds everything was hidden in a damp gray cloud. It was so thick that Leiv could not even see how big the floe he was standing on was. Then he heard a thunderous rumbling and the loud screams of people in distress, and animals bellowing with fear. He felt the floe he was standing on rise up until it was almost vertical, heard it collide with another. Then he was knocked over and was sliding down a steep wall of ice until he hit the freezing cold water. He had hardly gone under before another floe shot in under him and lifted him out of the water again.

There was a terrifying din on all sides. He heard the ice around him fragment with a series of ear-splitting cracks, the muffled boom each time the heavy floes collided, and he heard, too, the sound of splintering timber and knew that Thorstein's skiff would be crushed by the powerful masses of moving ice.

Then Leiv was thrown into the water once again. He gasped for air and kicked wildly with his legs to keep his head above water. When he came to the surface, a large beam was floating just alongside him. It was one of the beams to which the horses had been tethered in the hold. Three lengths of rope floated loose in the water, and in the fourth halter a horse was still bound. It was floating heavily and appeared to have drowned.

Leiv swam across and managed to get a grip on the beam. He dragged himself up onto it and, with fingers almost frozen stiff, managed to tie himself on with one of the empty halters. Once he was sitting securely, he could begin to look around. There was not much to see, however: nothing but floating ice closely packed around him. Everything else was obscured by the fog.

He shouted out loud, but there was no reply. For a moment he thought of cutting the dead horse free of the beam, but then he remembered that he might be in need of both skin and meat if he reached land.

Thorstein's skiff had been pressed under by the ice, Leiv was sure of it. Maybe the other two boats had gone down in the same way, and everyone on board was already dead. Leiv was so cold his teeth were chattering. He stretched out on the beam and tried to keep his skin boots out of the water.

How long Leiv rode on the beam dragging the dead horse after him, he did not know. From time to time he dozed, but only for a few brief moments. He did not allow himself to sleep for fear of rolling under the beam. There was no part of him that was not frozen stiff and weak with exhaustion, and he thought he would soon be dead. Then, later in the day, the sun broke through and dissolved the fog. Leiv lifted his head and looked listlessly around. First he looked out to sea. The ice had moved farther out, and he was floating around on his beam completely alone. The dead horse hung in the water. It had been caught by the current and was drifting toward the coast.

To his amazement Leiv realized that he was only a few hundred yards from a low, rocky coastline. He could see the foreshore, the rounded hills, covered by heather and willow scrub as well as the high slopes rising behind the coastline up toward a bluish ridge of everlasting snow. Leiv had reached Greenland.

5. The Boy on the Pole

The sudden summer storm did not take the Inuit by surprise. For them, it was entirely natural that winter weather could suddenly come along in the middle of summer.

When the storm had died down and Narua stuck her head out of the opening in the tent, she saw a thick layer of snow covering everything. The dogs had dug themselves in and were curled up tight, their snouts buried in their bushy tails.

But the winter weather did not last long. As soon as the sun broke through, the snow began to melt. Before the day was over summer returned, and the children cast off their warm clothes and ran around half-naked again.

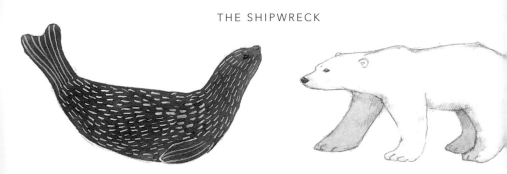

The day after the storm, the hunters went off looking for narwhal in an adjacent fjord. Apuluk, who could not yet row as far as that in his kayak, did not go with them. So he and Narua went up the mountain slope to catch king eider, which at that time of the year could not fly. The birds walked around with a bedraggled look, having completely lost the feathers that help them take flight.

Apuluk took with him his bird spear and a leather sling. Narua was carrying a large sack made of gut lining, in which they would place the birds they caught.

All the Inuit loved king eider. The juiciest tidbit is the little button of fat that grows on the top of its head. What they liked best was to eat this raw as soon as the bird was caught.

The children walked out to a headland that projected

44

a little way out to sea. From here they could see the
drift ice lying like a broad gleaming belt toward the
south. They knew that the field ice would continue to
lie like that for most of the summer, until the violent
autumn storms came and swept the sea clean. They
knew, too, how important it was that the ice remained
there, for under it there was a whole range of animals
to hunt — seals, walrus, narwhals, birds and bears. The
field ice was indeed a gigantic larder for the Inuit.

In one of the small valleys of the headland leading
off to the sea, Narua came upon the first group of king
eider. They were strutting around without a care in the
world.

Apuluk motioned his sister to go around behind
the birds. Narua sank down in the mountain heather
and wriggled on her stomach in a half-circle back

behind the place where the birds were. Once she had taken up position behind them and could lie looking down at them, Apuluk placed a stone in his sling, rose up and swung it above his head. The stone shot from the leather like a lightning bolt.

One of the king eiders was struck in the chest and fell in a heap, stunned. A second stone hissed from the sling. It whistled just past a large male, who seemed annoyed and shuffled a few feet to one side. The next stone hit its target and the bird dropped into the heather. Now Narua leapt up, and the flock fled toward Apuluk. They netted five birds in all. Proud of their haul, they seated themselves on a flat rock to enjoy the delicious knobs of fat while they were still warm.

As they were sitting there eating, Narua gripped her brother by the arm.

"Look out there!" she whispered. "What's that?"

Apuluk knelt up and shaded his eyes with his hands.

"It's a big pole. It's floating," he said. "But there's something lying on it."

"There's something behind it, too," said Narua, "something heavy floating in the water."

They hastily thrust the eider birds into the sack and ran down onto the beach.

"I think there's an Inuk lying on the pole," cried Narua breathlessly. "Look, it's trying to get up."

Apuluk nodded. He was standing right at the water's edge.

"It is an Inuk," he said. "We must see if we can help him in. I think he is floating over into that little inlet, over there."

From the small inlet they could see how the pole was gradually being drawn in toward the beach by the current. When the extraordinary craft was just half a dozen yards from the sandy shore, Apuluk waded out into the water. He gasped for breath as the icy cold enveloped his body.

It was not until he took hold of the pole that he realized that the Inuk was a boy. His hair was strangely fair and he had curious pale blue eyes.

The boy on the raft said something that Apuluk did not understand. He gestured with his arms, and Apuluk could see that he was tied onto the pole with a thick rope. Quickly Apuluk pushed the pole in toward the beach, and, once he and Narua had dragged it up onto the sand, they untied the rope.

For a moment Narua stood looking at the boy. Then she stared back at the water, where the dead horse lay lapping heavily against the water's edge.

"Apuluk!" she cried in terror. "There's a dead kilivpak lying there!"

Apuluk looked closely at the horse.

"It could be a kilivpak," he said, "or it could be an animal from the country the boy comes from."

He looked at the boy.

"I think he is one of the strangers father and the others saw last year at Simiutat."

"Do you think he is dangerous?" asked Narua.

She approached the boy. He was lying on his back shaking with cold. When her eyes met his, she could not help smiling. The boy smiled back.

"He smiles just like an Inuk," she said, "so he probably isn't terribly dangerous."

Apuluk kneeled beside the boy and began to peel his clothes off him. They were completely soaked in salt water and clung to his body. When he started to unbuckle the boy's belt with its large knife, the boy tried to stop him. But he was so exhausted from struggling to survive the cold that he was too weak to resist and his arms fell helplessly back onto the sand.

At last the strange boy lay there completely naked, and the two children looked at him in amazement. Never had they seen skin so white. It was almost, they thought, like the snow that had fallen the day before. His eyes were particularly remarkable. They were the same color as the water or the sky and quite different from those of an Inuk. This was an extraordinary boy they had fished ashore. But he looked quite harmless and, apart from his eyes, skin and hair, his body was formed like other Inuit.

"What are we going to do with him?" asked Narua. "Should we take him home to the settlement?"

Apuluk thought about it carefully. Then he shook his head.

"I'm not sure that would be a good idea," he answered. "The adults at home don't think much of these strangers. Maybe they will kill him, or send him out to sea again on his pole. Old Shili believes that these people are evil spirits, sent into this country to do the Inuit harm. He is a great shaman, and most of them will listen to him."

Narua nodded. She knew that Shili feared strangers more than anything. He was the tribe's shaman, and he had both experienced and seen things that were beyond ordinary people.

"What shall we do?"

"Maybe it would be best to find a cave where he can stay hidden for a time," said Apuluk. "There are some caves not far from here. They can only be seen from out at sea, so he will be safe there."

"But he can't stay there," retorted Narua. "It will be far too lonely."

Apuluk picked up the boy's knife and examined it.

"No, it will only be for a time. Anyway, I don't think we should take him to the settlement before we are sure that he is friendly and before he has learned some of our language. If he can speak like us, he will be able to explain to the elders where he comes from, what he is doing here and how he ended up on a pole out at sea."

Narua nodded.

"And then maybe they'll give him permission to stay with us. Oh! Isn't it exciting, Apuluk?"

The boy, who had not understood what the children were talking about, raised himself to a sitting position. He placed a hand on his chest.

"Leiv," he said in his own language. "My name is Leiv."

Narua looked at him inquiringly.

"Do you think he is hungry?" she asked.

"If he was, he would probably have rubbed his stomach or pointed at his mouth," said Apuluk. "But you can try to give him something."

Narua reached down into the sack and pulled out a bird, which she handed to the boy. He took it with a faint smile, but immediately laid it beside him. Then he pointed to himself again.

"Leiv, Leiv, Leiv," he repeated.

"I think he's saying his name," said Apuluk.

He pointed at the boy and repeated the word.

"Leiv," he said. "Leiv?"

The boy nodded eagerly. Then he pointed to Apuluk and raised his eyebrows questioningly.

"Apuluk," he replied, and pointed at his little sister.

"Narua."

"Apuluk, Narua," repeated Leiv quickly, and that made them laugh, all three of them, because the way he pronounced their names sounded so funny.

Once Leiv had torn the meat off the eider bird and swallowed it down, he started to pull on his clothes. But Apuluk took them from his hands and spread them out to dry on the rocks. Then he pointed to the animal in the water. Leiv nodded. He drew his knife out of his belt and together they walked down to the horse.

It was an enormous animal in the eyes of Narua and Apuluk, and at first they were a little frightened to touch it. But once Leiv set about cutting it up, they discovered that the animal was full of all the same things that were to be found in the animals they hunted, and their fear receded. It was just like any other animal, even though it did look rather strange, in the same way that Leiv was an ordinary Inuk who was just slightly different from the Inuit they knew.

By the time everything that was edible on the horse had been laid out in the sun to cure, Leiv's clothes were almost dry. He pulled them on and then began to tell the two Inuit children about his journey. They listened to him in silence and, even though they did not understand what he was saying, they perceived that this was something he wanted to talk about and that the things he had experienced had been terrifying.

Later that afternoon Apuluk and Narua took Leiv by the hand and led him to the caves where he was to remain concealed. They gathered heather and grasses, which they spread out in the largest chamber in the caves, and they made a couch where Leiv could sleep. Then they carried up the horsemeat so that wild animals

would not be able to get to it. They did not leave Leiv until late in the evening. Even though they could only exchange the four words that he had learned during the course of the day — fire, hunger, yes and no — it was as though they had known him for ages.

6. Acceptance

Leiv spent most of the summer in his cave. Narua and Apuluk visited him as often as they could. They had brought him a blubber lamp that he could use to cook his meat over. The lamp also kept him warm on cooler nights.

Leiv had other things to eat besides horsemeat. He fished for sea scorpion and polar cod along the beach and collected birds' eggs and berries, while the children brought him whatever juicy tidbits they could sneak from their mother's meat pot. But when Apuluk went hunting with his father and Narua had to help out at home, the days dragged for Leiv. It was only when his newfound friends were with him that time flew.

During the course of the summer months, Leiv learned enough of the Inuit language to make himself understood by Narua and Apuluk. It was not so difficult, he thought, even though many of their words were dreadfully long. Apuluk had thrown away Leiv's clothes, which were too worn and thin for life in the cold cave. Instead he brought Leiv a pair of his own trousers and an anoraq made of sealskin. Narua sewed a pair of sealskin boots for him and sealskin mittens that had a thumbhole on each side — which was practical when you had to slip them on quickly.

When the birds began to migrate southwards, Narua and Apuluk took Leiv with them to the settlement. He aroused great excitement. The children playing between the tents fled in horror when they saw him. They thought he was a spirit from the sea, dressed in Inuit clothes. Apuluk led Leiv to his father's tent, and it was not long before people from the other tents came streaming in to see the newcomer.

"We found him floating on a big piece of wood," explained Apuluk. "We dragged him on land and hid him in a cave until he had learned to speak a bit of Inuit language."

Apuluk's father considered Leiv carefully. He nodded several times but said nothing. But the old shaman, Shili, began to jabber.

"What have you done? Whatever have you done? Can't you see that you have brought misfortune to the settlement? This is a terrible spirit who has disguised himself as an Inuk!"

"Then we helped him do it," said Apuluk, "for both the anoraq and trousers are mine, and the boots were sewn by Narua."

"Be quiet, child!" hissed Shili, and he turned toward the hunters. "This is the familiar spirit of an evil man," he said pointing at Leiv. "He has been sent here to seek vengeance for something, but I do not yet know what."

Then Leiv spoke.

"I have not been sent by anyone. I come from a country called Iceland, a country that looks much like yours. And I wish you no ill."

He turned his gaze from Shili and looked toward Narua and Apuluk.

"These two are my sister, my brother," he said quietly.

Apuluk's father smiled. Leiv had pronounced the words all wrong, and several of the Inuit began to laugh. Then Apuluk's father spoke.

"You look like us but you are still different."

He approached Leiv and seemed to sniff him.

"But you have the scent of an Inuk."

Then old Shili began to shout.

"He comes from those terrible ships that sail around collecting Inuit to be eaten. You have all heard about the man from Katla's tribe who was sliced in two, haven't you?"

He leapt forwards, and started to dance wildly in front of Leiv.

"Kill him! Kill him!" he screamed.

Some of the hunters who believed everything Shili said tightened their grip on their long spears. One of them lowered his and aimed its point

at Leiv's head. Leiv saw it coming. He immediately placed a hand on the knife he was carrying in his belt and looked the man straight in the eye. Then he let go of his knife.

"No," he said. "There will not be blood between us as there was between my father and Thorstein."

At that moment an old woman, the children's aunt, stepped forward. She pointed toward the hunter with the lowered spear.

"Oho," she brayed, "now we can see what a great hunter really is! He has sniffed out big game. Look how his nostrils flare, like a fox who has found the spoor of a dying hare."

She laughed scornfully

"Why! Look at all the brave men we have in our midst! I'll say this much! And we women and children, we do feel safe, don't we? Just think, this great hunter is so brave that he dares to kill a defenseless child, a child who has done none of us any harm!"

Many of the adults in the tent could not help laughing at the old woman. And she did not stop.

"Oh, yes," she said, nodding her head. "It's not the first time old Shili has seen things that no one else has seen. Yet now he cannot even tell the difference between a real spirit and a boy from another country. He is too old, now. He should have taken his place out there on the ice and given his spirit to the winds long ago, as is the custom for a true Inuk."

Apuluk's father laughed.

"You are right," he said. "This boy is no spirit but an Inuk. My children have kept him hidden in a cave for a long time because they believed that we would kill him. Has he done them any harm? Does he not speak a bit of the Inuit tongue? Have we forgotten how to be hospitable toward those who visit us?"

He took a step toward Leiv and placed a hand on his shoulder.

"Since you have chosen Apuluk and Narua to be your brother and sister, I am minded to choose you as my son."

He looked about him, letting his gaze move slowly from face to face.

"This is my son," he said aloud, "sent to me by the mother of the sea, who holds in her hand the fate of all the creatures of the sea."

Leiv looked across at Narua and Apuluk, who were smiling and nodding at him. He had not understood everything their father had said, but he could see from the children that he had been accepted into the Inuit tribe.

7. The Three Friends

Leiv often thought of Thorstein and of all the people who had been on board the three skiffs. He was constantly combing the shores for flotsam or for some remnant from the crushed boats, but he never found anything. Either everything had sunk to the seabed or it had been carried further out to sea by the ice field and around the southernmost part of Greenland.

Once in a while he thought that he should perhaps break away from the Inuit and try to find one of the northman settlements he had heard being spoken about at home on Iceland. He knew that there was one called East Bay, where Erik the Red and his clan had lived, and that there was a West Bay that lay a little further north.

But he did not really have any desire to leave his friends. He had come to be very fond of Narua and Apuluk, and he admired their father and the other hunters for their skill when they were out at sea and on the hunt.

It did not take long for Leiv to learn to handle both harpoon and spears, and he soon became just as skillful as his foster brother, Apuluk. But that did not make Apuluk become envious. The more skillful Leiv became, the prouder Apuluk was.

The three children became inseparable. They were always together, scouring the uplands, where reindeer were to be found, and setting traps made of stone for foxes far from the settlement. The adults teased Narua, because she was always with the boys, but no one tried to keep her at home.

In winter, all three drove the same team of dogs, and on these trips Narua was indispensable to the boys. When they were out hunting or tending fox traps, she would remain back in their igloo or tent looking after the lamp, repairing their clothes and cooking. There was easily enough work for a girl who had to look after two hunters.

When they came home with their catch, Narua helped them skin and flense it, and could prepare the skins better than either of the boys. Narua was almost as skillful as a grown woman. They had a wonderful time together, the three of them.

Never had Leiv lived so free and unfettered a life. The only duty he had was to help find food, and that duty was more of a game for him. No one ever gave him orders, nor did anyone try to tell him what to do. And everyone was very friendly toward him. Even the old shaman, Shili, had grown fond of the boy from Iceland. For Leiv was always friendly toward the old man and often left a fine piece of seal meat or a delicious piece of liver outside the opening to the old man's tent.

During the course of the year that followed, Leiv taught himself to speak almost fluent Inuit. It came quite naturally, without his really having to do anything. To his surprise, he was suddenly aware that he could speak to his companions on the settlement as easily as he had previously spoken with people on Iceland.

For the Inuit, Leiv provided welcome new entertainment during the long winter nights. They could sit for hours listening to his accounts of life on Iceland. He also recounted all the things he had heard from his father about Viking expeditions to England and Ireland, and his stories of the king of Norway had the Inuit gaping in amazement. Only old Shili sat in a corner of the communal house rocking backwards and forwards and mumbling.

"Yes, yes. We know all about that kind of nobleman. Our countless journeys in the spirit world have taken us to many places like that."

Sometimes, Shili would replace Leiv and narrate Inuit sagas that were so fantastic it was Leiv's turn to gape in astonishment. When old Shili grew tired and fell asleep in the middle of a story, the children's grandfather took up the tale, for he knew the sagas just as well as the shaman.

By the time the second winter had come around,

the tribe had moved a good way north of the place where Leiv had drifted ashore. That winter Apuluk, Narua and Leiv accompanied the adults on the hunt. It was a prosperous winter with plenty of meat.

The following summer they journeyed with the heavily laden umiak further north to the summer settlement that lay near Simiutat. Leiv knew that they were only a few days' journey from the northman settlement, but he had no real desire to leave the tribe. The life that they led suited him very well, and he could not imagine being without Narua or Apuluk.

Apuluk and Leiv were now in their fifteenth year. They were both powerfully built and almost as strong as grown men. Narua, who was fourteen, had become rounder and more womanly. But her brown eyes still brimmed with warmth and laughter, and she would giggle playfully whenever the boys teased her.

The boys often engaged in trials of strength. They arm-wrestled, finger-wrestled or simply wrestled the way Leiv had learned on Iceland. But oddly enough neither of them ever walked away triumphant. Narua laughed at them and said that one did not want to beat the other, for their friendship was too strong for that. And that is probably the way it was.

One day in the late autumn, the boys and Narua went on a hunting trip out onto the periphery of the ice sheet. They drove right out to the sea and pitched camp close to the water's edge. When they had erected a light tent of skin and upturned the sled so the dogs would not run off with it, they lay down, tired after their long journey.

It had been an exhausting trip, during which they had had to drive through soft snow and icy meltwater lakes where the water came right up over the boards of the sled. Leiv lay in his sleeping sack of reindeer skin. He could feel the ice rocking beneath him.

"I hope it doesn't give way," he murmured anxiously. "It's a bit thin out here, isn't it?"

Apuluk pulled his hood over his face.

"Yes," he replied. "It is thinner than usual. But it'll bear up all right. Sea ice is tougher than the ice on the lakes."

Narua said nothing. She had fallen asleep the moment she crept into her sleeping sack.

But the ice did not bear up. In the middle of the night they were woken by a loud crack, and all three sat up in sudden fear.

"What was it?"

Leiv crawled out of his sleeping sack.

"I think it was the ice splitting," replied Apuluk.

They stumbled out of the tent and saw that the ice had indeed fractured. A long tongue of water separated them from the solid ice sheet and the safety of the coast. The crack was too wide for them to jump across. Narua gripped Leiv by the arm.

"Can you swim?" she asked. "Neither Apuluk nor I know how to."

Leiv nodded.

"Tie the harpoon lines together," he said, "and I'll try to swim across to the sled and the dogs."

Apuluk and Narua helped each other to tie the long harpoon lines together, while Leiv undressed.

Once he was standing naked on the ice, they tied

the rope around his waist and, with a piercing shriek, he threw himself into the water. With long strokes he began to swim across to the solid ice, while Apuluk paid out the line after him. Narua's eyes followed Leiv

anxiously, her hands clenched tight, as Leiv was halted by the line just a few yards short of the ice. Leiv tried to shout something to them, but he was so far gone with cold that his shouts were no more than indecipherable screams. Apuluk saw how Leiv was sinking lower in the water, saw his arms become weaker and his strokes begin to fail.

"Haul him in!" he shouted to Narua, and together they pulled Leiv quickly back to the ice floe. By the time they got him out of the water he was half-dead with cold. They dragged him into the tent and stuffed him into the thick sleeping sack. Narua put blubber on the lamp and began boiling soup from the carcass of a gull.

"It was a good thing you didn't let go of the line," stammered Leiv.

He was so cold that his teeth were rattling.

"I could never have managed the last bit, would never have got up onto the ice."

Apuluk nodded. He knew that the waters around Greenland were very dangerous and that people could only survive in them for a few moments before they got cramped and sank to the bottom.

"You'll have something hot soon," said Narua. "Then you'll stop shivering."

The ice floe on which they found themselves was taken by the current and pushed slowly northwards. Now and then Apuluk looked out of the opening of the tent and eventually the solid ice sheet had dwindled to a thin white line.

Leiv had regained some warmth by drinking Narua's soup. One of his feet was extremely painful, but he said nothing to the others.

"What'll happen to the dogs now?" he asked.

Apuluk tied up the opening.

"When they get really hungry, they'll bite through the traces and eat them. Then they'll run home."

Narua put out some of the wicks in the lamp to save blubber.

"Then Father will realize that something is wrong, and the hunters will drive out to look for us," she said.

"But that could take a long time?" Leiv was looking at her.

She nodded.

"It could," she said quietly. "But perhaps we will drift in to land before they find us."

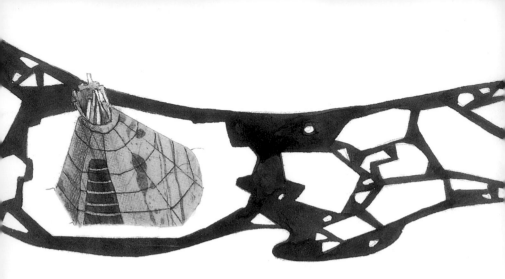

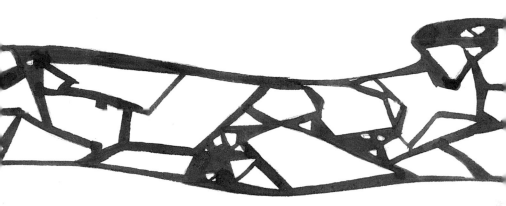

8. On the Ice Floe

Leiv's foot grew worse and worse. Narua saw that he was in great pain and insisted that he remove his hareskin boot and show her how bad it was. The whole foot was very swollen and two of the toes had already turned blue.

"Geruneq," she whispered to her big brother, and Apuluk looked down at Leiv, his eyes full of sorrow.

"What is it?" Leiv had never heard the word before.

"Frostbite," answered Narua. "It's making your foot go rotten."

"Can you do anything about it?"

Apuluk knelt down and looked at Leiv's toes, which were now almost black.

"Yes," he answered. "The only thing to be done is

77

to cut out the blackness. Then the rest of the foot may recover."

Leiv stared up at the skin of the tent.

"Use my knife," he said. "It's the sharpest."

Apuluk drew the knife out of Leiv's sealskin boot. He wiped it on a patch of hareskin and sat on top of Leiv's knee.

"Hold his hands," he said to Narua.

"You don't need to do that," replied Leiv.

But Narua took one of his hands between both of hers and gripped it tight.

When Apuluk made the first cut into the healthy flesh behind the black toes, an excruciating pain shot through Leiv. He groaned between clenched teeth and flung his head from side to side. But the weight of Apuluk's body held his leg still. Narua was holding his hand so tightly her knuckles turned white.

Apuluk cut around the bone of the rotting toes and with a little crack broke first one toe off and then the other. A couple of spasms passed through Leiv's body. Then he lay completely still.

Narua let go of his hand and placed small tots of hareskin soaked in urine on the wounds and bound a long strip of skin tight around his foot.

Some moments later Leiv awoke. He groaned with pain and looked up at Apuluk.

"Is it over?"

"Yes. Both of them have gone."

"Will I get well now?"

"I think so. The rest of your foot looks healthy enough, apart from the fact that you'll lose all the skin."

Narua held a bowl of soup out toward Leiv.

"Drink some of this." She smiled. "This soup was made out of one of your kinsmen."

"Kinsmen?"

"Tateraqen, the three-toed gull."

As luck would have it, after they had slept six times on the ice floe the current swung in toward land. They were propelled quite close to a promontory of low, snow-covered mountains, and Apuluk calculated that one end of the ice floe would collide with land before the current swept it out to sea once more.

Quickly they packed up their tent, tied the sleeping sacks together and helped Leiv over to the tip of the ice floe that would strike the coast. Narua had wound a sealskin around Leiv's injured foot and even though it was dreadfully painful, he was able to put his weight on it by putting his heel on the ice first.

It worked out as Apuluk had thought it would. The tip of the ice floe swung slowly in toward the coast, and they could cross from the ice up onto land without difficulty. It was a wonderful feeling to have firm ground beneath their feet once more, and they decided to find a way up to one of the valley beds and pitch camp there. Apuluk walked ahead with two sleeping sacks and the tent. Leiv had his arm around

Narua's shoulder. He was carrying his own sleeping sack, and Narua had a large skin bag with cooking things.

Once they had found a favorable

spot and raised the tent, Apuluk wanted to make a fire. Narua handed him the little bag with the fire drill, the bow and dry moss. He knelt down and placed the dry  stick in the bow so that the tip rested in a square piece of wood. Then he began to draw the bow so that the stick spun around. Faster and faster it went, and from the heat that came out of it there soon arose a thin column of smoke. Narua carefully pushed the dry moss in toward the smoke, little by little while Apuluk continued to spin the drill. When the first tiny glimmer appeared, Narua lay down and blew, making the light grow and spread. Soon the moss was burning with small, clear flames.

Apuluk was dripping with sweat. It was hard work making fire, and Leiv gazed at him in admiration. Only when the fire was burning strongly did Apuluk erect a frame of polar birch, from which Narua could suspend her pot. That evening they ate sea scorpion that Narua had caught in the tidal crack. It was a welcome change from the dried seal meat they had consumed for days on the ice.

"It's a funny thing," said Leiv when all three of them were lying in their sleeping sacks, full and warm, "but we northmen always call you 'Skrællinger.'"

"What are 'Skrællinger'?" asked Narua.

"Well, it's a put-down word. It means something like 'weaklings,'" Leiv explained. He could not help smiling at the thought. "I don't know why northmen think you Inuit are weak and stupid, for you know much more than we do."

He poked his head out of his hood and looked at Apuluk.

"If I had been alone now, I would have drowned on the ice floe, died from the rot in my foot or frozen to death. I can't even make fire, you know."

"We have always lived up here," Apuluk said modestly, "and maybe that's why we have learned to get by here a little bit better than your people."

82

"Have you really always lived in ice and snow?" asked Leiv. "Haven't you ever had a winter without snow, like we sometimes have on Iceland?"

Narua laughed.

"A winter without snow would be awful. That would mean you couldn't drive dogsleds or build igloos. It must be terrible to live on Iceland."

Leiv shook his head thoughtfully.

"When I think about how we lived back home, I can't understand how you manage to keep yourselves alive up here. You have got no animals apart from the dogs — no cows, no sheep, no horses. Without them I don't think we could survive on Iceland. You've just got the sea and what it can give you."

"But it gives us everything we need," replied Apuluk. "Seals are the most important. They give us food and clothing. Walrus give us thongs, skins for boot soles and meat. Reindeer give us warm sleeping sacks, anoraq and delicious meat. From bears, we get meat for both dogs and people, and we can sew trousers out of their skins or use them as sleeping skins."

Narua interrupted.

"We have everything up here, everything anyone could need. Think of the birds. Of their lovely eggs, of the fine coats we can sew from their skins and feathers, of the little auks we preserve in blubber and keep for use in winter. We have hares, which we use to make stockings and small pairs of trousers, fox furs to keep us warm and protect us from the wind, and musk ox, which have the finest meat you can eat. Oh yes, there really is everything up here! What are cows and sheep and horses compared to such richness?"

Leiv nodded.

"You are right. What more could one want? My Uncle Helge wanted an awful lot. He went out into the world to find a mass of things he didn't need at all."

"What things?" asked Narua.

"Gold and silver and expensive clothes and things like that," replied Leiv.

"What are gold and silver?" asked Apuluk curiously.

"Well, they are metals. Like the iron my knife is made of but just much finer."

"So maybe he wanted to make knives out of it?"

Leiv laughed.

"No, it's no good for that. You make jewelry out of it."

"What is jewelry?" Narua turned on her side and rested her head on one hand.

"It's something you hang around your neck or put around your wrist or wear on your fingers."

"Why would you do that?"

"Why? Because it looks good, I think."

"Does it?" Narua wanted to know.

Leiv shook his head.

"I'm not at all sure about that anymore. But it was for all these things that my Uncle Helge went off and killed people."

"Did he kill people?" Apuluk looked at Leiv in astonishment, "to get this metal to put on his fingers?"

Leiv nodded.

"Yes, I think it's strange now, too. Do you kill people?"

"Yes," answered Apuluk, "but only when it has to be done. If we kill a person, it is because they do not deserve to live and are possessed by a very evil spirit."

He drew his hood away from his face.

"There was once a hunter in the tribe," he said, "who was not on good terms with Sila."

"What is Sila?"

"That is hard to explain." Apuluk looked questioningly at his sister.

"Sila is everything. Sila is in everything. In the mountains and in the skies, in the ice, the stones on the beach and in all animals. Everything is Sila. Do you understand?" explained Narua.

Leiv nodded. "It is probably a kind of god," he said. "Or perhaps like all the gods together. But why didn't this hunter get along with Sila?"

Apuluk continued.

"It's hard to say, but it was as if Sila wanted nothing to do with him. He was always unlucky. With his hunting, with his family, with the ice and the weather. Everything went against him. And then he grew sad and did evil things to other people. He just couldn't stop himself from killing, and it was all because Sila had abandoned him."

"Did he start killing people for no reason at all?"

"No. There was a reason," answered Apuluk, "for he was deeply saddened by this thing with Sila. But soon after he had murdered three good hunters, the other adults thought it was necessary to stop him. So they killed him and bored a small hole in his forehead, so the evil spirits could fly out."

Leiv turned in his sleeping sack, the pain in his foot making him give a stifled groan.

"But do you really never go to war?" he asked.

"I don't know what that means," replied Apuluk. He repeated the word that Leiv had said in Icelandic.

"What does 'war' mean?"

Leiv pondered. It was a long time before he spoke.

"War is a quarrel between people. When some

people want to have something other people have, there is war. Then people keep killing each other until the strongest wins."

Narua stretched out on her back again and looked up at the roof of the tent.

"We have never had war," she said. "But maybe that is because the people up here do not have so much. Here we share everything and do not crave what others have."

"I am glad," murmured Leiv just before they drifted off to sleep. "I am glad that I am living with you. I have learned to live as Inuit do."

"Sleep now," Apuluk replied drowsily. "We have a long way to go tomorrow."

9. The Bear

The next day, the three friends began to walk in the direction that Apuluk believed would lead to the northman settlement. They climbed to the top of the ridge, skirting the spot gouged by the current where they had beached with the ice floe, then they turned back again to the solid ice sheet. This time, however, they reached the coast. Leiv had one arm around Narua's shoulder and used a harpoon as a cane.

They made only slow progress. It was warm, the sun shining from a clear sky. The early autumn snow, which had lain on the uplands and on the ice, melted and created small lakes that they were constantly forced to skirt.

That day Apuluk harpooned an seal in an ice hole. They were all very hungry and they ate the liver while it was still warm and raw, before cutting the remainder of the meat into long strips. Apuluk bound the meat with a thong and dragged it after him as they continued on their way.

Suddenly Apuluk noticed bear tracks. He knelt down and examined them carefully.

"It's not long since it walked by here," he said. "Its spoor is very fresh. I hope it hasn't got wind of us. Our weapons are no match for a bear."

To check that the bear had moved on, Apuluk and Narua each crawled up an outcrop of ice and scanned every quarter. There were no bears to be seen. The tracks led toward the sea and disappeared in some narrow lakes.

"It must have gone out to the edge of the ice sheet," said Apuluk when he returned. "There are lots of seals out there at this time of the year."

But the bear was not on the edge of the ice. It was an elderly she-bear, who had seen the children and smelled the seal meat. She had hidden among some outcrops of ice and was keeping a close eye on what the three humans were doing. The bear was hungry. She was old and it was difficult for her to catch seals. Once in a while she could outwit a young and inexperienced seal, but such meals were few and far between. She lay motionless and watched the humans approach. It was only when they were a few yards away that she leapt out at them, roaring.

Terrified, the children stopped in their tracks.

"Run!" shouted Leiv. "I'll try to stab it with my knife."

Apuluk threw down his pack and grabbed the harpoon Leiv was carrying. In no time, he had strung the sharp point and was aiming it at the bear.

"It's no good running," he said. "It'll catch us in no time."

"Throw the meat out for it!" suggested Narua.

"Stay where you are!" shouted Apuluk. "I'll try to harpoon it when it leaps."

Leiv nodded. He drew out his long knife and held it up toward the bear.

But the animal took her time. She was sure of her prey — this would be easy. Slowly she moved in closer, so close they could hear her hoarse breathing. Leiv had never seen a live bear before. The bears that had been brought to the settlement had always been dead, and they had looked peaceful, friendly even. But this old bear was monstrous. Its mouth hung half-open, its long fangs glistening yellow, saliva dripping over its leathery black lips. Its ears were sharp with excitement, and its eyes, bloodshot with fury.

"When it crouches, I'll throw," whispered Apuluk.

The bear stopped a short distance from the children. It arched its back and was just about to launch into a powerful leap when Apuluk slung his harpoon at it with all his might. The sharp tip of the harpoon sank deep into its neck and the shaft broke off and fell onto the ice.

Stung by the harpoon, the bear roared in agony. The wound was unpleasant but it was not fatal. The hurt animal gripped the harpoon line with its huge paws and tried to rip the weapon out of its neck. When it finally drew out the bone harpoon tip, blood shot from the wound in a bright jet.

"I think it's cut through an artery!" Apuluk shouted, triumphant. "Look at all that blood!"

The bear was snarling like a mad beast. It gathered itself in an awkward leap and landed on top of Apuluk, who had failed to throw himself far enough out of the way. But Leiv lifted his knife and sprang right into the arms of the bear. It clutched him between its forelegs and sunk its teeth into his shoulder.

"Stab it!" screamed Apuluk.

Apuluk was pinned under the bear's hindquarters, unable to move. But Leiv could not stab. The bear was holding his hands locked in a grip of iron.

Narua had been watching the fight, paralyzed with fear. But when she saw Leiv locked in the bear's embrace, she was so furious that she forgot to be frightened. Quickly she gathered up the shaft of the harpoon and hammered the bear's head with it again and again. Surprised, the bear turned and lashed out at this new attacker with one great paw. That was just the opportunity Leiv was waiting for. He angled his arm and drove his knife right into the bear's heart.

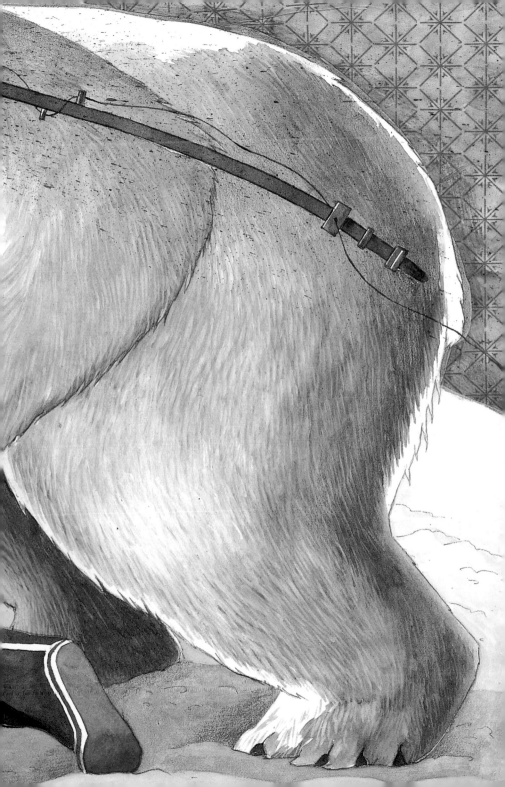

For an instant the bear stood there, swaying. Then it coughed once, twice. The fiery redness drained from its eyes and with a strange gurgling sound it fell forwards, carrying Leiv with it in its fall. The massive body twitched a couple of times, then lay still.

It took a long time for Leiv and Narua to roll the dead beast off Apuluk. When they got him free, they realized that he was unconscious. Narua examined him but found only a few minor injuries. Leiv was bleeding from the shoulder where the bear had fixed its teeth. They were deep, round wounds that Narua bound up with strips of skin. While she was treating Leiv, Apuluk came to. He twisted onto his side and screamed in pain.

"My leg! There is something wrong with my leg!"

Carefully, Narua took off his boot and slit up his trouser leg with Leiv's knife. The bone was broken. It must have happened when the bear dropped its hindquarters onto him. The fracture looked ugly. The lower part of the leg was at a strange angle and a fragment of shinbone protruded a little under his knee.

"It's broken," said Leiv. "We shall have to set it or you'll never walk properly again."

Apuluk nodded. He gave a crooked smile.

"Now it's your turn, Leiv. I shall do my best to be just as uncomplaining as you were."

Leiv cut up the bear. From under its huge chest he broke off two ribs. Then he returned to Apuluk.

"This is going to hurt," he said to prepare him.

Apuluk did not answer. He turned his head so that his cheek rested against the snow and closed his eyes. Leiv took hold of the broken leg. He pulled the two halves apart and tried to get the ends of the bones to meet. Not a sound came from Apuluk. He lay with his eyes tight shut. Only his compressed lips spoke of the extremity of his pain. Once Leiv felt that the bones were set right, he placed a bear rib on either side of the break and held them firmly while Narua bound harpoon line tightly around both leg and splint. When they had finished, she carefully pulled Apuluk's leggings back into place, then cut open the top of his sealskin boot and drew it over his foot.

Narua and Leiv spent that night making a sled out of the bearskin that they could drag behind them. Shortly after the sun had risen, they rolled Apuluk onto the sled, loaded their sleeping sacks and cooking utensils on the rear of the skin and then resumed their long journey.

They made only slow progress. Leiv was in great pain and still had difficulty placing weight on his foot. But Narua was tireless. Not for one moment did she lose her good spirits. Even though it was she who toiled the hardest, they never heard a complaint pass her lips. Leiv often thought that had it not been for Narua, both he and Apuluk would have died long before.

Every evening they broke their journey to sleep for a few hours. Leiv and Apuluk got the fire going, while Narua gathered brushwood to feed it. They had little to eat. A few frozen berries that Narua found, a little seaweed and on separate occasions a sea scorpion and a cod that she fished out of the tidal cracks.

But one evening she came back to the camp and announced she had spotted a herd of reindeer. They

were grazing on a bank leading down to a dry river-
bed, and she was certain they had not caught her
scent.

Apuluk proposed that she and Leiv should try to
sneak up on them. If they were really lucky there might
be an old animal that had difficulty keeping up with
the rest of the herd.

The reindeer were grazing where Narua had said,
and they crept up on them carefully and slowly.

"There are no old animals among them," whispered
Narua, disappointed.

Leiv gazed hungrily down at the deer.

"See if you can crawl behind them," he said. "If you
can chase them toward me, I might be able to hit one
with my knife."

Narua nodded and immediately began to creep
around behind the reindeer. She wormed her way
through the heather but, even though she tried to be
as silent as possible, dry twigs cracked beneath her.
Reindeer have very sharp hearing and they began to
look uneasily up the bank. Narua lay completely still

She saw how the animals stood as though frozen in position, and how they eagerly sniffed into the wind. Then all of a sudden she heard a whistling sound, followed by a dull thud and saw a large reindeer leap high in the air before falling lifeless to the ground. She looked over toward Leiv. He was on his feet, staring up the bank. She sprung up and ran across to him. But before she reached him, Leiv began running down toward the dead reindeer as quickly as his bad

foot would allow. He was waving his knife wildly in the air and was shouting a word she did not understand.

"Thorstein! Thorstein!"

10. The Boy Who Wanted to be Inuk

Narua's eyes wandered curiously around the big house. She was sitting on a narrow bunk where Leiv's tribal kinsmen had laid Apuluk. The house was larger than any she had ever seen before. There was an enormous room where all these people lived, and this room extended into a lower building, where they had their animals locked in small pens.

She listened to the many foreign voices and thought how dreadfully frightened she would surely have been, if Leiv had not been there.

Thorstein of Stockanæs listened with interest to Leiv, as he spoke of his rescue and his time among the

Inuit. It was only when Leiv had finished that he spoke.

"You have told us much about this people, whom we have always called 'Skrællinger'," he said, "and I think we have learned something from your story. Now I'll tell you what happened to me out on the ice three years ago."

And then Thorstein told the story of his own incredible escape. His skiff had been pressed under by the ice but not as quickly as they had expected. There had been time to lower both his people and the animals onto the ice. As luck would have it, they had lain right up against a very large ice floe that had withstood the pressure from the floes surrounding it.

The two other skiffs had been badly damaged but remained afloat even though many planks had been crushed. Once the storm had abated a little, the boats were hauled in toward the ice floe on which Thorstein and his crew had taken refuge, and they were taken on board.

After that they had sailed to West Bay, where they had repaired the boats. About two years ago they had found this valley, where they had built the farm, which was named Stockanæs after the one they had left behind on Iceland.

When Thorstein had concluded his story, he reached a hand out to grip Leiv's arm.

"You have grown," he said with a smile. "Your arms will soon be just as long as mine."

Leiv blushed faintly. He could remember their agreement.

"They're not quite there yet," he mumbled, "and I doubt they'll ever get that long."

"There will be peace between us," said Thorstein, "and there will be peace between us and your Inuit friends."

He rose and unbuckled his sword. Then crossed over to Apuluk, drew the sword from its sheath and held it out to him.

Apuluk took it. He studied it closely, feeling the sharp edge of its blade, weighing it in his hands. Then handed it back with a shake of his head.

"Tell him that it is his," said Thorstein.

But Apuluk continued to shake his head.

"It's no use to me," he said to Leiv in Inuit. "It is far too big and heavy, so it would be better if he kept it."

"Inuit don't use swords," Leiv explained, "for they never go to war. Give him a knife, Thorstein. He can use that for hunting."

Thorstein laid his sword on the table and drew out his knife. Apuluk's broad smile told him that this was a fitting gift.

"What would the girl like?" he asked Leiv.

Leiv looked at Narua. She was sitting gazing at Apuluk's knife with shining eyes.

"Is there anything you want, Narua?"

She shook her head without answering.

"There must be something you would like," Leiv insisted. "Would you like a knife, too?"

"No."

Narua looked across at one of the women sitting at the table sewing.

"Perhaps a needle like the one she's using?" she said.

Leiv translated, and Thorstein roared with laughter

He reached across the table, took hold of the woman's sewing box and laid it in Narua's lap. She looked up at him, dumbfounded by his action. Then she opened the box and took out one needle. Having examined it carefully, she hid it away under her black topknot. Then she explained to Leiv that a needle like that was a fabulous gift. It was an incredible needle that could be sharpened time and again and could probably last the rest of her life. She only needed one needle for she could not sew with more than one at a time anyway. Thorstein took the sewing box back thoughtfully and returned to sit at the table.

"An interesting people." His voice was a deep rumble. "And in many ways, a people to be admired."

He looked at Leiv.

"Hmm. Well, I guess you'll be staying here, on Stockanæs, Leiv?"

He grasped his sword and buckled it around his waist.

Leiv looked at the sword, and suddenly he had a feeling that he was gazing back into an evil and senseless past. Then he looked at Narua and Apuluk and felt himself flooded with an overwhelming joy.

"No," he answered. "But I shall stay on Greenland."

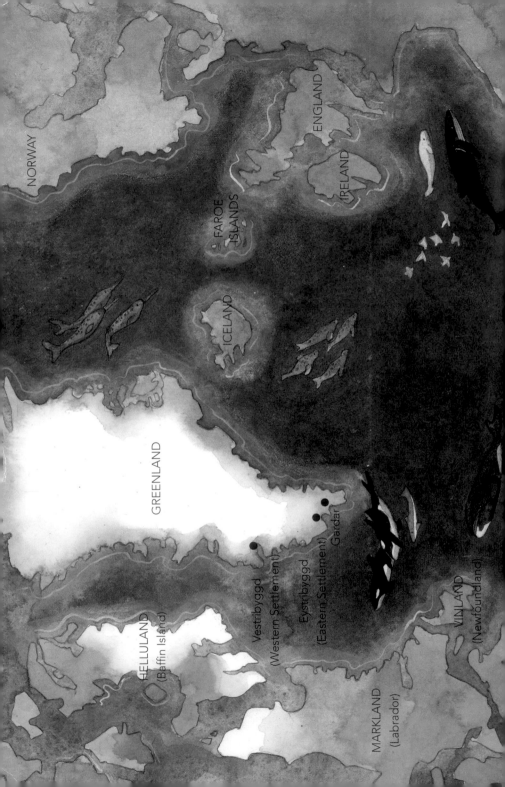